My name is _____

and this is my

Healing Hearts Club™

Story & Activity Book

AMERICAN BIBLE SOCIETY

HEALING HEARTS CLUB BOOK
STORIES AND ACTIVITIES FOR CHILDREN

© 2013 American Bible Society

ISBN 9781937628901
ABS Item 124164

For use with:
Healing Children's Wounds of Trauma: Facilitator's Book (ISBN 9781937628932, ABS item 124167)
by Harriet Hill, Margaret Hill, Debbie Braaksma, and Lyn Westman

This book is intentionally written in basic English.

Unless otherwise noted, Scripture quotations are taken from the
Contemporary English Version © 1995, 2006 American Bible Society.
Bible stories are adapted from Scripture.

Design: Peter Edman
Illustrations: Ian Dale

**For training in how to use this book to carry out trauma healing,
see your local Bible Society, visit TraumaHealingInstitute.org,
or write to traumahealing@americanbible.org.**

AMERICAN BIBLE SOCIETY
1865 Broadway
New York, NY 10023

CONTENTS

Healing Hearts Club Book

LESSON 1: I AM IMPORTANT TO GOD

Am I important to anyone?

"Come on! Race you to the river!" Sami called to his friends. It was early evening, and a whole group of children were getting water for their mothers. They ran around the twisting muddy path to the local stream. "I'm here first!" shouted Sami, and rushed into the stream to be the first to fill his bucket with water. Back they all raced to the village, hoping to have time for a game of football before their parents gave them some other jobs to do.

As the children ran back into the village, they noticed that something was going on. A group of men were talking together in the market area. Although it was time when the women normally would have been cooking the evening meal, a number of women were sitting outside the church.

Sami ran home with his water bucket and left it in the kitchen. He looked around for one of his older brothers and found his sixteen-year-old brother, Setu, leaning against the door with a frown on his face. Sami asked him, "What's going on?"

"Oh, you're just a kid! You wouldn't understand! Get out of my way!" Setu said as he pushed past Sami and went into the house.

At this point, Sami's sister, Rose, came back with some firewood for the kitchen fire. Rose was looking frightened. Sami asked her, "What's happening?"

Rose replied, "I don't know! The women told me to go away because I'm too young to understand, but I think something bad is going to happen."

That night everyone in Sami's compound was eating their evening meal under the trees and the adults were talking in whispers. Sami's father kept going into the house to listen to his radio.

Sami, who was eleven years old, tried to ask his parents some questions, but he was told to be quiet. Rose, who was nine years old, didn't even try to ask anything because no one had listened to her earlier. As they went to sleep that night, they were a bit afraid. Both children were thinking that no one cared what they thought or said. As Sami drifted off to sleep, he thought, "It would be nice to think that someone really loves and cares about me—to know that I am important to someone." But he didn't sleep for long because suddenly, in the middle of the night . . .

This is a picture of me.
I am important and special to God.

Creation
Genesis 1 and 2

Before God created the world, only God was there. No one created God. He was always there. At the beginning when God was ready to make the world and the entire universe, there was just a shapeless mass, confusion, and darkness.

On the first day, God spoke light and darkness into being, and said, "It is good!"

On the second day, God made the water and the sky.

On the third day, God brought the waters on earth together to make oceans and seas. Then he spoke, and all kinds of trees and plants appeared. Each tree had its own seeds that could make another tree just like the first. As God looked at all the things he had created, he said, "It is good."

On the fourth day, God made the sun to shine in the day, and the moon and many stars to shine in the night, and he said, "It is good!"

On the fifth day, God made all the winged birds and the swimming fish. Each one was different, and he said to them, "Go and multiply until you fill the water and the sky." And again, God said that all these things he made were good.

On the sixth day God made many different kinds of animals, like dogs and cats, horses and cows, elephants and giraffes. He also made the creeping crawly things like lizards and spiders. He made all the animals different from each other, and each one could have babies that would be the same as the parents.

Then God made the most amazing thing of all! He made a man and a woman. He said to them, "Have many children so that you and your family will spread out over the earth." The man and woman were very special, different from the animals, because God made them to be like himself. When God had finished, he looked at everything he had made, and he said, "It is very good!"

Then God rested on the seventh day from all his work.

God created the universe

Draw what God created each day.

1 Light and darkness	**2** Sky and water

3 Land, seas, plants, and trees	**4** Sun, moon, and stars
5 Fish and birds	**6** Animals and humans

Memory verse

Genesis 1.31a: "God looked at what he had done. All of it was very good!"

LESSON 2: WHY DO BAD THINGS HAPPEN?

The Fall
Genesis 2 and 3

The two people that God made first were named Adam and Eve. God put them in a beautiful garden and gave them the job of caring for all the plants and animals in the garden he had created. The only rule God gave them was not to eat from the tree of the knowledge of good and evil. He warned them by saying, "You may eat the fruit of any tree in the garden, except the tree that gives knowledge of what is good and what is bad. You must not eat the fruit of that tree; if you do, you will die."

One of the creatures in the garden was the snake, who was really Satan. He always wants to defeat God and rule creation in God's place. He is always disobeying God, lying, and doing bad things to hurt people. So the snake came to Eve and asked her, "Did God really say that you could not eat from any of the trees in the garden?" Eve answered, "We may eat the fruit of any tree in the garden except the tree in the middle of the garden. God told us not to eat the fruit of that tree or even touch it; if we do, we will die." The snake said, "That's not true; you will not die. God said that because he knows that when you eat the fruit of that tree, you will see what you have done and know what is good and what is bad."

Eve wanted the fruit so she ate some and also gave some to her husband Adam. Then Adam and Eve realized they were naked, and began to be afraid. So when God came to walk with them in the garden that evening, they hid from God. When God asked why they were hiding from him, Adam said, "We are naked so we hid." God said, "Who told you that you were naked? Have you eaten of the tree I told you not to eat?" Adam blamed Eve, saying, "It was the woman you gave me who brought me the fruit and I ate it." Then God said to the woman, "Why did you do this thing?" And she said, "The snake tricked me and so that is why I ate it."

Bad always results from doing something wrong. God told the snake he would have to crawl on his stomach, and he said that there would be hatred between the snake and the woman. God also promised that many years later, someone from the woman's family would crush the head of the snake. This means that this person would defeat Satan. God then told Eve that she would have pain when giving birth to children, and that her husband would rule over her.

God said to Adam that he would have to work very hard to care for the land and grow food. Yet God still loved Adam and Eve very

much. They were special to him even though they sinned, so God made clothes for them from animal skins.

After that God sent both of them out of the garden, and he placed living creatures and a flaming sword which turned in every direction at the front of the garden. This stopped them from ever coming back into the garden.

Memory verse

> Psalm 147.3: "God renews our hopes and heals our bodies."

Wake up! Run, quickly!

Suddenly, in the middle of the night, Sami and Rose's parents rushed around waking their children. They told them to grab anything they could, because they all had to run quickly out of the village. Sami's parents, Lambo and Judit, ran out of their house with their six children and an old uncle.

As they ran, they could hear gunshots and could see that some of the houses were being set on fire. Through the darkness they could see men dressed in uniforms, running around the edge of the village.

As they ran into the bush, Sami turned around and saw that his old uncle was running very slowly, and was behind the rest of the family. As Sami looked, he heard a shot and he saw his uncle drop to the ground. Sami's father yelled to his family, "Come on!"

It was a dark night with only a tiny bit of light from the new moon. As they ran through the trees, Sami's family got mixed up with some of the other families from the village. Suddenly, some

men with guns appeared from behind the trees in front of them, and started shooting at them while they were running away.

In all the confusion, Sami got separated from his family. He ran and ran until he was far away from all the noise and shooting. After a while he met up with another group of people who had escaped from a different village, and he joined them. When the group decided they were probably safe, they stopped and tried to rest for a while, sleeping under the trees.

As Sami was lying there, he began thinking, "What is going to happen to me now? How can I find my family again? How is my uncle? Who are these bad men who came into the village to kill us and burn down our house? The pastor says that God loves us, so why did he let these bad people come?" Sami's head ached with all these thoughts, but finally he fell asleep.

Feeling faces

Draw a happy face and a sad face.

Happy Face	Sad Face

LESSON 3: SAYING HOW WE FEEL

Rose feels bad

The rest of Sami's family had managed to stay together, and they were still wandering around trying to find him. Finally they decided they had to stop and rest. As they settled down, three other families from the village joined them. Some of the women were wailing and crying. The men were trying to make them be quiet because they were afraid that the rebels who had burned down their village would hear them.

Sami's sister, Rose, was happy to see the family of one of her good school friends, Jana. Rose went over to look for Jana, but quickly realized something was wrong because she could not find her. Finally Jana's older brother told Rose that as his family ran out of the village, one of the rebels shot Jana and killed her. He said that they couldn't even bring her body along because the rebels would have shot anyone who had gone back for it.

Rose ran back to her own family and curled herself into a tight ball, leaning against a tree. She felt so numb, so very upset, that she couldn't even cry. After a while her mother came over to comfort her.

At first Rose wouldn't speak to her mother, but finally she burst out with some angry questions. Rose asked, "Why did those bad men shoot and kill Jana? Why did they kill our uncle? We didn't do anything to them! Why did they come and hurt us? And where's

Sami? He's probably dead, too! It's not fair!" Now both Rose and her mother were crying, and all her mother could do was to hold her tightly.

After a few hours, the sun rose and the families started to talk about what to do next. Rose's father, Lambo, was the natural leader of the group since he was a village elder. He sent a couple of the young men to see if they could find Sami, and to see if there were any traces of the rebel soldiers.

They came back some hours later and said that the group needed to stay where they were because rebels were all around them. The young men had also found a field of ripe maize (corn) just beyond where the group was hiding and had brought some food for everyone. Lambo had had the good sense to bring some matches in a plastic bag, so they were able to start a fire. Everyone was still very frightened and shocked, but they also knew they needed to prepare for the night by making shelters.

My lament letter

Dear God, it is not fair that . . .

_____

_____

_____

_____

_____

_____

_____

_____

_____

_____

_____

_____

_____

_____

_____

_____

Joseph and his jealous brothers
Genesis 37

At the end of our last story, God sent Adam and Eve out of the beautiful garden. They had children, and their children had children until there were people living all over the world. The story you are going to hear today happened many years later.

The Bible story of Joseph begins when he is about seventeen years old. He was watching his father's animals with his brothers. When Joseph came home, he told his father about the bad things his brothers had done. Jacob, the father, loved Joseph more than his other sons and made him a very beautiful and colorful coat. When the brothers saw that Jacob loved Joseph more than he loved them, they hated Joseph and would say mean things to him.

Joseph had two special dreams. In the first dream, Joseph and his brothers were tying bundles of grain together, and suddenly the brothers' bundles gathered around Joseph's bundle and bowed down to it. In Joseph's second dream the sun, the moon, and eleven stars were bowing down to him. Because the dreams showed that Joseph would rule over his family one day, Joseph's brothers were jealous of him and hated him even more.

Some time later, Jacob sent Joseph to look for his brothers. When the brothers saw him coming they made plans to kill him. "Here comes that dreamer!" they said to each other. "Come on! Let's kill him, throw his body into one of the dry wells, and say that a wild animal killed him. Then we will see what becomes of his dreams!"

In order to save Joseph's life, Reuben, his oldest brother, suggested that they throw Joseph into the well, but not kill him. He planned to rescue Joseph secretly later on. He knew that if anything happened to Joseph, he would be held responsible. But while he was gone, some traveling traders came by and Judah and the other brothers decided to sell Joseph to them.

After the traders had taken Joseph away, his brothers took his coat and dipped it in goat's blood. They took it back to the father, telling him that a wild animal had killed and eaten Joseph. Jacob was very, very sad. He tore his clothes and mourned for Joseph, saying that he would mourn for his son Joseph until the day he died.

So Joseph's own brothers sold him for twenty pieces of silver to some traders. They took him to Egypt and sold him as a slave to Potiphar, an important man. So Joseph, frightened and sad, began to live far away from home and family.

Draw Joseph leaving for Egypt looking sad and frightened

Memory verse

Psalm 62.8: "Trust God, my friends, and always tell him each of your concerns. God is our place of safety."

LESSON 4: FEELING LONELY

A new home

While his family was looking for him, Rose's brother Sami was getting further and further away from them. Sami was with a group of people who had decided to try to walk to the next country where they thought they would be safe. The adults in the group tried to be kind to Sami, but they were more concerned about looking after their own children. When they found food, Sami was often the last person to get a share.

On and on they walked, day after day. Two small babies died from fever. After a short service, their bodies were buried beside the path, and the group continued walking. Sami felt very lonely, even though he was with other people. He worried about what had happened to his own family. He wondered if maybe they had all been killed.

Sami also worried that he might get sick and die. He thought that no one really wanted to look after him, that he was just a stray kid tagging along with the group. He felt like an orphan. By this time he was getting very thin and tired. One big kid, in particular, treated Sami like a slave. Every time he refused to carry something or do a chore, this boy would beat him. Sami became very angry inside because of this bad treatment.

After three weeks of walking, the group finally crossed the border into the next country, Sanatu. Now they felt safe, but they still needed somewhere to stay. After a couple of days, the group arrived in a large town and the police sent the group to a refugee camp. They were taken to a reception center where a woman asked them their names and other information. When Sami gave his information, the woman realized that he was a child without a family, so she made plans for him to be taken to an orphanage right away.

Sami felt awful as he was taken by truck to the orphanage. The group he was with hadn't always been very kind to him, but at least they were from the same area and spoke the same language. He thought, "Where am I going now?" He felt lonely and frightened.

My important memories

Important memories

Important memories

Important memories

Joseph in Egypt
Genesis 39

In the last lesson, we learned that Joseph had been sold as a slave by his brothers and taken by force to Egypt. But even though his family abandoned Joseph and his whole life changed overnight, he was successful because the Lord was with him. Potiphar, the Egyptian leader, put Joseph in charge of everything he owned.

Joseph was well built and handsome and Potiphar's wife asked him to go to bed with her. Joseph refused to do this. He said that this would not be right because Potiphar had given him responsibility for everything and trusted him. Joseph also said that he couldn't sin against God! Day after day Joseph refused Potiphar's wife.

But one day when no one else was in the house, she grabbed him by his robe and demanded, "Come to bed with me!" Joseph left his robe in her hands and ran out the door. Potiphar's wife then accused Joseph of trying to rape her. She said that when she screamed he ran outside, leaving his robe beside her. When Potiphar heard his wife's story, he became very angry with Joseph and put him in prison.

Joseph was rejected by his own family and sent away. And now, once again, the people he cared about lied about him, rejected him, and put him in prison. But God was still with Joseph and showed him kindness. The warden of the prison saw that he was a good person. So Joseph was put in charge of all the prisoners and was responsible for all that happened in the prison. The warden trusted Joseph to do his job because the Lord was with Joseph and gave him success in all he did.

Memory verse

Hebrews 13.5b: "The Lord has promised that he will not leave us or desert us."

LESSON 5: BUILDING OUR LIFE WELL

No family

Sami was with three other boys in the truck as they traveled towards the orphanage. "What do you think it will be like?" Riki, a young scared-looking boy of eight, quietly asked. The oldest boy in the group replied, "Prison, I should think! High walls, nothing much to eat, hard work! You'll see!" By the time they drove up to the gates of the orphanage the children were shivering with fear, from hunger, and from not having enough clothes. As the truck entered the compound, they saw a number of nice looking houses. Flowers surrounded all the houses along with some vegetable plots. In the distance they could see a playing field.

The orphanage director came to welcome the boys as they climbed out of the truck. They were taken into an office and had to answer some questions. All the information about them was carefully written down. After the director had finished questioning Sami, he said, "Well, it looks like the first thing you need is a long bath, some new clothes, and a good meal! Tomorrow we'll have the doctor look at you, and treat those nasty sores on your legs."

Sami was taken to one of the houses and introduced to the house-mother. She said, "Welcome to your new home. Let's get you a bath and some clothes. Then it will be time for dinner and you can meet the other children who are here." Sami sat down to his first good meal in a month, feeling comfortable and clean, and dressed in good clothes. He could hardly believe what had happened.

Sami quickly settled down in the orphanage and enjoyed being with the other children. Each day they went off the compound to a local school. Sami enjoyed being back at school again. However, some of the children there were unkind to the orphans. They teased them by saying things like, "Your parents didn't like you, and so they got rid of you, didn't they?" Sometimes at night, Sami had nightmares, and woke up crying for his parents.

Building a wall

Write down good things you need in your life and bad things you don't.

GOOD BRICKS
I need in my life

BAD BRICKS
I will not use
to build my life

Joseph: forgotten once more
Genesis 40

In our last lesson, Joseph was thrown into prison even though he hadn't done anything wrong. Every time things started going better for Joseph, it seems like something bad happened!

Some time after Joseph was put into prison, the king's steward (who served drinks to the king) and the king's baker both offended the king. They were thrown into the prison where Joseph was. Joseph was told to care for them. After a while, on the very same night, both men had a dream.

When Joseph saw the two men the next morning, they were very sad and depressed. Joseph said to them, "Why do you look so worried today?" They told Joseph that they each had dreams, but no one could tell them what the dreams meant. Joseph said to them, "It is God who gives people the ability to interpret dreams. Tell me your dreams."

The steward told Joseph that in his dream he saw a vine that produced three branches of fruit. The steward squeezed the fruit into the king's cup and put the cup in his hand. Joseph told the steward that in three days, like the three vines, the King would give the steward his position again. Then Joseph said, "But please remember me when everything is going well for you. Please be kind enough to mention me to the king and help me get out of this prison. After all, I was kidnapped from the land of the Jews, and while here in Egypt I have done nothing to deserve being put in prison."

When the baker saw that Joseph gave a good explanation to the steward, he asked Joseph to explain his dream, too. The baker told Joseph that in his dream he was carrying three baskets of bread on his head, but some birds were eating the bread out of the top basket!

Joseph told the baker that the three baskets were three days, and that in three days the king would have the baker put to death.

Three days later was the king's birthday, and he gave a feast for all of his officials. He brought the steward and baker before the officials. Then the king gave the steward back his previous job, but he had the baker put to death, just as Joseph had said. Even though Joseph had helped him, the steward never gave Joseph another thought. He forgot all about him, and didn't say anything to the king about him.

Draw the baker's dream

Memory verse

Jeremiah 29.11 (GNT): "I alone know the plans I have for you, plans to bring you prosperity and not disaster, plans to bring about the future you hope for."

LESSON 6: LOSS AND GRIEF

Life in the forest

Back in the forest, Sami's family had settled down into a routine. They built shelters from sticks and grass. One old man in the group knew how to weave sleeping mats. He taught everyone how to do this. They learned to pile up grass and leaves and put them under the mats to make their beds more comfortable. Fortunately, it was harvest time for a number of crops. Groups of men were able to go and harvest the crops, often during the night so the rebels wouldn't find them.

There was a stream running near where they were staying, so they were able to drink water that was fairly clean. Everyone had learned to fish, and the children had lots of fun catching little fish. While the children were fishing for little fish, the adults worked hard to trap some of the big ones. Rose still thought about her little friend, her missing brother, and the uncle who had been killed, but at least now she was beginning to play with the other children.

Every morning the little community started the day with prayer and reading the Bible, though at the beginning some people refused to join in. They said that God had left them, so they wouldn't pray. People were getting enough to eat, and as time went on they learned ways of making their lives a bit more comfortable.

However, there was one real problem. They had no medicines and no means of getting them. But there was one old woman who knew about plants that helped cure certain sicknesses. Every time anyone became sick, the whole group prayed to God with their whole hearts and asked for healing. Rose started having nightmares; she dreamed that she would die like her friend Jana had died.

After about a month, Rose's father, Lambo, decided it was time to find out if it was safe to go back to their village. He sent a couple of young men to find out. Just after they left, Lambo's wife, Judit, fell ill. She had a high fever for two days, and then she died suddenly. At almost the exact moment of her death, the two young men came back to say that the United Nations had set up a camp for displaced people. The United Nations said that they should all come out of the bush and stay at the camp for now. Lambo was beside himself with grief and anger. He kept saying, "If only I had sent those men sooner, we might have been in the camp and could have found medicine for Judit. Why did God allow this?"

Rose cried and cried, and wouldn't be comforted. One of her brothers didn't cry at all, but kept saying, "She's not really dead! She'll wake up soon!" Lambo and the children buried Judit there in the bush, and tried to mark the grave so that they would be able to find it again. Then they set off to the camp for displaced people.

My losses

This is the road of grief. If you have lost someone you love, mark where you think you are today on the road. Also mark where you would like to be in one year's time.

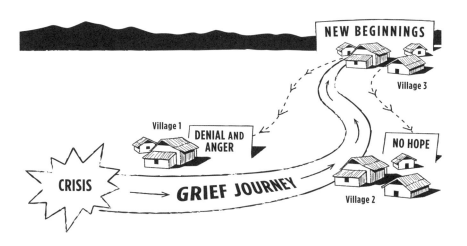

Joseph is still in prison
Genesis 40–41

In the last lesson, Joseph was still in the prison. The steward, whose dreams Joseph had explained, forgot him. Some time had passed, and Joseph must have thought many times about how difficult life was for him.

Some of the times in Joseph's life were good, and then he could have hope for his future. One of those times was when God gave him the meaning of the dreams and the steward was set free. The steward should have remembered Joseph, but he didn't. And now Joseph was still alone, locked in prison, still remembering. Joseph thought to himself, "If only my brothers hadn't hated me; if only Potiphar's

wife hadn't lied about me; if only the steward had remembered me."
Thirteen years is a long time to think about all that you've lost.

Two full years passed before Joseph's life changed. At that time,
the king of Egypt had two dreams that troubled him very much. In
both dreams, the king was standing by the Nile River. In the first
dream, there were seven fat cows that were eaten by seven thin and
ugly cows. In the second dream, there were seven healthy heads of
grain that were swallowed up by seven thin heads of grain. Then the
king woke up. He was worried, so he sent for his wise men and magi-
cians, but none of them could tell the king what his dreams meant.

Finally, the steward remembered Joseph. He told the king that
Joseph had explained two dreams in prison correctly. So the king sent

for Joseph. He asked Joseph if he could explain his dreams. Joseph answered, "I cannot, Your Majesty, but God will give an explanation." After the king described what happened in his dreams, Joseph told him that they were both the same dream. Joseph explained that there would be seven years in Egypt with good harvests. These seven good years would be followed by seven years of drought and famine. Joseph told the king that he should store grain during the good years to feed the people during the seven years of poor crops and famine.

The king was so impressed with Joseph that he put Joseph in charge of his palace and all the people. Only the king himself was greater than Joseph! The king then gave Joseph a woman to be his wife, and they had two sons before the years of famine. Joseph organized storehouses all over the country where they collected grain.

Then the years of famine came. The famine affected Egypt and all the neighboring countries. Hungry people came from everywhere to buy grain from Joseph.

Memory verse

Psalm 10.14: "But [God,] you see the trouble and the distress, and you will do something. The poor can count on you, and so can orphans."

LESSON 7: BAD TOUCH

Joy tells Rose a secret

After walking for a couple of days, Rose's family finally arrived at the camp for displaced people. Each family was given a tent to stay in. Each month, they lined up to receive their rations of food. They enjoyed having better meals, but they didn't enjoy being crammed together with so many other people. Often quarrels and fights broke out because people were tense and unhappy.

There was a school at the camp, and all the children were supposed to go each day. Rose had enjoyed school before the rebels came, and had been quick to learn. Now, however, she didn't want to go to school. When her father made her go, she was very quiet and didn't speak in class. The teacher didn't really take much notice of her. He was more concerned about the children who had become naughty and behaved badly in class.

As time went on, Rose's father recovered from the shock of his wife's death and started to feel like himself again. He was able to help his children talk about everything that happened and how they felt about it. As Rose was able to say what was going on inside her, she started feeling better and began to join in more in the activities at school.

Rose had a good friend in her class named Joy whom she knew from her village. Rose thought that Joy had changed a lot, and wondered why. Before the rebels came she had been a happy, bouncy girl, always ready to have fun. Now she was very quiet and seemed bitter towards other people. She also seemed very frightened of men.

One day Rose and Joy were by themselves gathering mushrooms near the camp. Rose suddenly asked Joy, "Why are you so different now?"

Joy didn't answer for a while and then slowly and quietly she replied, "Something bad happened when we were out in the bush." Rose asked, "You mean, you were sick?"

Joy said, "No, it's about my uncle."

Rose asked, "Did he beat you?"

Joy said, "No, it was different from that . . . and now I feel dirty and bad. My uncle touched me in places he shouldn't touch, on my private parts. It hurt and I do not know what to do. He's still living in the same tent with us, and I'm afraid whenever he is around that he will do it again."

"I'm so sorry," Rose said. Then she asked, "Did you tell your mother?"

"No!" exclaimed Joy. "My uncle said he would beat me if I told anyone!" Rose was rather puzzled by all of this and worried for her friend. Her parents had told her that if anyone was really hurting one of her friends, she should tell them.

Rose's father, Lambo, had one of his sisters staying with them to help look after the children, and Rose liked this auntie very much. That evening they were alone outside cooking supper, and Rose told the auntie what Joy had said. The auntie didn't say very much, but after the children were in bed, they could hear her having a long discussion with their father.

The next day Lambo went to see Joy's father. The following day, Joy's uncle wasn't there anymore. Joy's mother spent time with Joy that night, and told her that it was the right thing to do to tell her friend Rose about what happened with her uncle. She also told her it was never the fault of the child when these things happened, but always the fault of the adult. Joy cried for a while and then they prayed together that God would heal the pain inside.

After a while Rose could see that Joy was looking much happier. She wasn't like she used to be, but at least they could have fun together again.

A flower to color

When you feel dirty, God can heal you and make you like a new flower again. Color in this flower and draw some more.

Joseph is in charge

Genesis 42–44

Now let's see what was happening with Joseph's family where they were living in the neighboring country of Canaan. Remember that Joseph was in charge of looking after the food in Egypt. Joseph had an important job because there was a famine, and this was the only food for all of the neighboring countries.

When Joseph's father, Jacob, learned that there was food in Egypt, he told ten of his sons to go to Egypt to buy some so that they would not starve to death. Jacob did not send Benjamin, the youngest son, because Jacob was afraid he might get hurt.

When Joseph's brothers arrived in Egypt, they bowed down to Joseph since he was responsible for selling the grain. The brothers did not know that this was Joseph because they had not seen him for many years. But Joseph knew who they were. So in an angry voice Joseph asked his brothers where they came from. They told him they came from Canaan. Then Joseph accused them of lying, and of being spies. The brothers exclaimed, "We are not spies! We are all the sons of one father; one brother is still at home and one has died."

Then Joseph put them in prison for three days, and finally let all of them leave except Simeon, one of the brothers. Joseph said, "When you come back with your youngest brother, then Simeon can come out of prison. If you don't bring your youngest brother, I won't sell you any more food!"

The brothers said to one another, "Now we are suffering because of what we did to our brother. We saw the great trouble he was in when he begged for help, but we would not listen. That is why we are in this trouble now."

The brothers didn't know that Joseph could understand them. He had been using an interpreter (someone who can translate from one language to another) so they thought he didn't know what they said. But Joseph did that just to fool them. He heard everything they said and had to turn away because he was crying.

So Joseph secretly put their money back in their bags and sent his brothers on their way. They returned home and told Jacob all that had happened. They told him what Joseph had told them to do. Jacob did not want to send Benjamin back with the brothers. He was afraid that Benjamin would not return, just like Joseph and Simeon. But when all the grain was gone, Judah knew that they had to go back to Egypt with Benjamin, or they would all die. So Judah promised Jacob to protect Benjamin or take the blame, and the brothers returned to Egypt.

When the brothers returned to Egypt, Joseph invited them all to dinner in the palace. The brothers were frightened, but they joined Joseph, along with Simeon, for dinner. When Joseph saw Benjamin, he was so overcome with feelings he had to rush out and go to his room to cry. Finally, when he was able to control his feelings, he returned to the dining hall and told all of them to eat. Joseph gave Benjamin five times as much food as he gave the other brothers.

After the meal, Joseph sent the brothers on their way. He put their money back in their sacks—but he also had a servant hide his silver drinking cup in Benjamin's bag. After a while the servant came running after the brothers, and said, "You are thieves!" When all the sacks were opened, the cup was found in Benjamin's sack! They went back to the palace, and Joseph demanded, "The one who stole my cup will be my slave now."

Judah explained to Joseph all that his father Jacob had said. He explained how Jacob was afraid that something would happen to Benjamin, which would cause a great amount of grief to Jacob. Judah then said, "And now sir, I will stay here as your slave in place of the boy; let him go back with his brothers. How can I go back to my father, Jacob, if the boy is not returned? I cannot bear to see this disaster come upon my father."

Memory verse

Isaiah 43.1 (GNT): "The LORD who created you says, 'Do not be afraid—I will save you. I have called you by name—you are mine.'"

LESSON 8: TAKING OUR PAIN TO THE CROSS

Rose asks Jesus to be her friend

From the time they arrived in the camp, Lambo had been asking about Sami, but no one seemed to know where he was. The local leaders had looked for him in the other refugee camps in the town, but he was not there. No one knew that, in fact, Sami was in a different country!

Rose often thought about her brother and prayed that God would bring him back. However, since the rebels had come to the village, she had only prayed occasionally about anything. Rose really didn't expect God to answer her prayers because God had let her mother die. In her heart, Rose didn't trust God anymore.

One Sunday there was a pastor who came to the church in the camp. This pastor said he wanted to talk to the children. He explained that sin came into the world when Adam and Eve disobeyed God, and that was why bad things happened—not because God was weak. He said that since we're all children of Adam and Eve, we sin, too, even if we don't mean to.

The pastor told the story of Joseph, and how his brothers were jealous of him and sold him to traders. One bad thing after another happened to him, but he didn't give up. He continued to believe that God loved him and that God would help him. Then the pastor said that thousands of years after Joseph died, God sent his own son,

Jesus, to live in the world and die on the cross. When he died on the cross, he took our place as a sacrifice for all the sins of the world, and for all of the pain and suffering that has come from those sins.

Rose listened carefully to what the pastor was saying. At the end of his talk, he said, "Let's thank Jesus for coming to live and sacrifice his life for our sins. Would any of you like to ask Jesus into your lives, to be your friend and forgive you for your sins? Would any of you like to bring the pain in your heart to Jesus and ask him to heal it? Think about it."

Sitting outside the tent that evening, Rose talked to her auntie about what she had heard that day. Her auntie said, "When I was a little girl, even younger than you, my father died and my mother was very ill. I felt like nobody cared about me. One day in church, I asked Jesus to come into my life, forgive my sins, and be my friend. I wanted to obey and please God as my loving father. Then I felt peace inside me and I knew that God loved me. When other bad things happened in my life, I always knew Jesus was with me, no matter what."

Because of all that had happened to Rose, Jesus seemed very far away from her. Now she wanted him to be close to her. So after some time, she said to her auntie, "I want Jesus to come into my life and be my friend." They prayed together and Rose felt a peace she had not known even since before the rebels had come.

The Road of Life

Where is Jesus on your road?

Jesus came to deliver us from sin and suffering

We learned that when Adam and Eve disobeyed God in the garden, people began to suffer. But remember how God told the snake that someone from the woman's family would crush his head—that is, put an end to Satan's power? God's people waited for a very, very long time for this promise to come true. Many people lived their whole lives without seeing this happen. God sent messages to his people through the prophets to keep telling people that someday this promise would come true.

Finally, it happened! The prophets said that a son would be born in the town of Bethlehem. And that is just what happened. Jesus was born in Bethlehem to a young girl named Mary. When he grew up, he went around the countryside teaching the people about God, healing the sick, and doing other miracles. He was especially kind to children.

He listened to them, touched them, and healed them even when the adults tried to push them away.

In the end, some leaders were jealous of how popular Jesus was, and they arranged to have him killed by the government. Jesus was nailed to a cross and died a very painful death. He was dead for three days, but then he came back to life. He appeared to his followers to encourage them, and to let them know that he was sending the Holy Spirit to help them. He promised he would come back again one day. Then he went up into heaven.

When Jesus died, he took the sins and the suffering of the whole world on himself. This is why we can take our pain to the cross and ask Jesus to forgive our sins and heal our wounded hearts. Jesus crushed the power of Satan and sin.

Memory verse

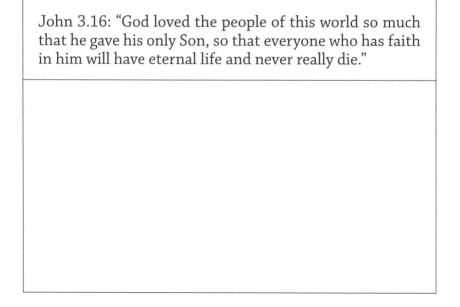

John 3.16: "God loved the people of this world so much that he gave his only Son, so that everyone who has faith in him will have eternal life and never really die."

LESSON 9: FORGIVENESS

Sami has a hot stone in his stomach

Back in the orphanage in Sanatu, Sami was growing quickly. He fit in well with the other children and he had many friends. Sometimes, however, he had angry and bitter thoughts. He was angry with the rebels who had made him lose his family. He was angry with the boy who had tried to make him his slave in the bush. He was angry with his family because he thought they weren't trying to find him. He was even angry with God who had let these horrible things happen. When he thought about these things, sometimes he had a stomachache or a headache. It was like something burning inside him.

One evening, he was sitting outside with those angry thoughts, when the housemother came out. She saw Sami sitting there all alone so she came and sat down beside him. The housemother asked, "What are you thinking about, with such a frown on your face?"

Sami replied, "I want to get big and strong so that I can go and fight the boy who beat me! I'd like to kill him, and the rebels, too!"

The housemother asked, "Does it make you feel better to think like that?" Sami said, "No, it makes me feel like there is a hot stone in my stomach!"

The housemother asked, "Do you know that Jesus loves you so very much? He wants to be your friend. Do you know that Jesus wants to forgive you for all of the bad things you have done and heal the wounds you have in your heart?"

Sami replied, "No! I don't think that Jesus would want to be friends with me because I am not a good boy. I don't think he can forgive me because I'm so angry with many people—and with him, too."

The housemother said kindly, "It's normal to feel angry, Sami."

Sami looked at her and said, "I'm supposed to forgive them though, aren't I? To be friends with Jesus I'm supposed to forgive the rebels and that boy . . . and I don't want to. I don't think I can!"

The housemother was quiet for a moment, thinking about what he had said. Then she said, "Sami, what do you think it means to forgive someone?" Sami looked at her. He had never thought of that question. He wasn't really sure what the answer was. Then he said, "To forget about the bad things someone did to you? To say it didn't matter?"

The housemother shook her head and said, "No, Sami, because what happened to you does matter. And you can't forget it just like that. What happened to you matters to me, and to you, and it really matters to God. Forgiving is not forgetting and saying it doesn't matter. It is saying, "You hurt me, but I am not going to hate you anymore. I am not going to try to pay you back." You see, God does not say to us that the wrong things we do don't matter. They mattered enough that Jesus died because of them. But God says he still loves us, and wants to be our friend, so he won't make us pay for those things. He did that himself, you see, when he died for us.

Sami pounded his fist against his knee. "I just don't think I can forgive them! I want to be friends with Jesus, but I don't think I can stop hating them! I want to hurt them because they hurt me."

The housemother said, "Sami, try being friends with Jesus first . . . you don't have to forgive them to be friends with Jesus. He wants to be your friend, whether you forgive or not. But when we are friends with him, that's when he helps us learn how to forgive.

Sometimes it can take a long time to forgive people who have hurt us. That's part of the journey of following Jesus."

Sami was quiet for a little while. What the housemother said made sense. He looked up and said, "OK—maybe if I'm Jesus' friend, he can teach me how to forgive. Maybe he can help me not be so angry. I want to be Jesus' friend."

"Let's tell him, then," said the housemother. And they did.

Letting go

Draw Sami tied to the boy he won't forgive. Then draw him free.

Joseph and forgiveness

Genesis 45

After Judah said that he was willing to become a slave so that Benjamin could go home to his father, Joseph could no longer pretend that he did not know and love his brothers. He sent the attendants away. He cried very loudly and said, "I am Joseph! Is my father still alive?" But his brothers were not able to answer him because they were very afraid! Then Joseph told the brothers to come close to him. He said, "I am your brother Joseph, whom you sold into Egypt! Now do not be upset or blame yourselves because you sold me here. It was really God who sent me ahead of you to save people's lives."

Joseph told his brothers to go home and tell his father what had happened to him. He told them to bring Jacob and his entire family and their animals to Egypt so they would be saved from the famine. Joseph knew that there would be five more years of famine. Joseph threw his arms around Benjamin and both of them cried. He kissed all his brothers and wept with them, too.

When the king heard the news he was pleased and sent the brothers off with carts to bring the family back. He promised to give them the best land in Egypt. Joseph sent his brothers away with gifts and nice food, but gave even more to Benjamin. As the brothers were leaving, Joseph said, "Don't quarrel on the way!"

When the brothers returned to their father, Jacob, they told him "Joseph is alive! He is ruler of all Egypt!" Jacob didn't believe them at first, but when they explained all that Joseph had said and showed him all that he had given to them, Jacob recovered from the shock. And then Jacob said, "My son, Joseph, is still alive! This is all I could ask for! I will go and see him before I die."

Memory verse

Matthew 5.44: Jesus said, "Love your enemies and pray for anyone who mistreats you."

LESSON 10: REBUILDING LIVES

Good news!

One morning, just at the beginning of the rainy season, Rose woke up in the refugee camp. She could hear loud, excited voices outside the tent. She was frightened and wondered if the rebels were coming to attack them again.

But almost before she had finished thinking this, her father, Lambo, came into the tent with a big smile on his face! He said, "Good news! The authorities have just told us that we can return to our village. And they're giving us tools, seeds, and some money to help us rebuild the houses and plant the fields." All the children shouted and jumped up and down, saying, "We are going home! We're going home!"

That whole week they were busy getting ready to return to their village. At the end of the week, one of Lambo's friends came over holding a radio. He said, "Did you know that the UN has found some children from our area in Sanatu? They are going to read a list of the names of the children on the radio in a few minutes. I thought you might want to listen in case that's where Sami is."

Lambo replied, "Well, I can't imagine how he could be so far away, but let's listen anyway." The whole family gathered around to listen to the radio. The announcer read out a long list of names, and suddenly, near the end, they heard Sami's name! The tent nearly blew away with the screams and yells of joy from the group.

Lambo rushed off to the camp office to ask how they could contact the orphanage and get Sami back. The office people were happy to hear the news. They promised that by the time the family was back in the village, they would find a way to bring Sami to them.

The next week passed in a whirl of activity. Everyone was busy! The families packed their belongings into a large truck and traveled back to their village. Some of their joy turned to sadness when they saw that their village had been burned and completely destroyed. Lambo said, "There's going to be a lot of work for all of us. But God is with us, and we can rebuild the village—and our lives as well!"

A week after they arrived back, a small truck drove into the village, and a boy climbed out. For a moment, no one recognized him. Then they screamed, "It's Sami!" He had grown a lot and looked older, but underneath he was still the same Sami. Sami had been told that his mother had died, but hadn't really taken it in. He couldn't believe it was true. When Sami saw his family and his mother wasn't with them, it became real to him that he would never see her again. So the reunion had feelings of sadness and happiness at the same time.

Later in the week, Sami and Rose were collecting wood for the fire and began to talk. They both shared their stories of how they had asked Jesus into their lives to be their friend. This was a very special time, and they both realized that there was so much they didn't know yet about their new friend Jesus.

Sami said, "We need to learn more about Jesus. They taught us a lot at the orphanage, and I'll tell you some of it. I hope they rebuild the church soon so that we can hear more about God there, too. Life isn't going to be easy, but at least we are not alone anymore. Jesus will always be with us."

Draw a picture of yourself feeling relaxed

Joseph's family is reunited
Genesis 46–50

Now Jacob was full of joy, and yet he was afraid as well. Then God spoke to Jacob in a dream, and told him not to be afraid to go to Egypt. At Jacob's request, Joseph met Jacob and all his families on the way. When Jacob and Joseph finally met, Joseph threw his arms around his father's neck and cried for a long time. Jacob said to Joseph, "I am ready to die, now that I have seen you and know that you are still alive."

Then Joseph went to the king to ask for land for his family, and the king granted some of the best land to Joseph's family. The famine was still very bad, and there was no food except that which had been stored by Joseph. So Joseph provided for all the people and saved them from death. Jacob was now 130 years old, and he lived for another seventeen years in Egypt.

During that time Jacob's family, called the Israelites, became rich and had many children. At 147 years old, Jacob became ill and was dying. Jacob told Joseph that one day God would take him and his descendants, his great-great-grandchildren, back to their own land in Canaan. Jacob then called all of his sons together and told each one what the future would hold for them. Jacob told his sons the place in Canaan where he wanted to be buried. Then he died. Joseph threw himself on his father, crying and kissing his face. They mourned his death and then they took his body to Canaan and buried it there. When they finished, they came back to Egypt.

But then Joseph's brothers said, "Now that our father is dead, what if Joseph still hates us and plans to pay us back for all the harm we did to him?" So they sent a message to Joseph, "Before our father died, he told us to ask you, 'Please forgive the crime your brothers committed when they wronged you.' Now please forgive us the wrong that we, the servants of your father's God, have done." Joseph cried when he received this message. Then his brothers themselves came and bowed down before him. "Here we are before you as your slaves," they said.

But Joseph said to them, "Don't be afraid! I can't put myself in the place of God. You plotted evil against me, but God turned it into good. He did this in order to preserve the lives of many people who are alive today because of what happened. You have nothing to fear. I will take care of you and your children." So he reassured them with kind words that touched their hearts.

Joseph lived to be 110 years old. When he was about to die, Joseph made his sons promise that when he died, they would carry his body back to Canaan with them. And 430 years later, when Moses led the Israelites out of slavery in Egypt, they remembered the promise that was made to Joseph, and took his bones with them to freedom.

Memory verse

> John 16.33: "I have told you this, so that you might have peace in your hearts because of me. While you are in the world, you will have to suffer. But cheer up! I have defeated the world."

Trauma Healing Institute

TraumaHealingInstitute.org